I0770131

Chével Nelson
New York, NY

Author's Note: This is a work of fiction. Names, characters, places, and incidents are a product of the author's imagination. Locales and public names are sometimes used for atmospheric purposes. Any resemblance to actual people, living or dead, or to businesses, companies, events, institutions, or locales is completely coincidental.

Magnificently you. Real life reminders that you are magnificent just as you are. /
Chével Nelson -- 1st ed.
ISBN 979-8-9857104-3-4

Dedicated to all those that struggled remembering who you are.

You are not alone.

"I pray you chose
joy.
Anything else is a
waste of time."

— Dr. Sonia Waters

Contents

Foreword By Jeanine Johnson-Smith 12

Advice 19

Waiting 21

Silence............ 23

Growth............ 25

Intentional 27

Conviction 29

Why? 31

Power 33

Random Thoughts........... 35

Two days............ 37

What about me? 39

WTH!!........... 41

Uncomfortable........... 43

A season of brokenness......................46

Exhaustion 48

Ambition 50

F**k around and find out...............53

Perception of me 56

Tiny Little Invisible Cuts.................58

Strong = Burden.............................61

Hamster Wheel...............................64

Time 66

Masterpiece...................................68

Begging 70

Control is a façade..........................72

Nothingness 75

Grace 77

Backwards......................................79

Clutter...81

Heavy 84

Running 87

Energy 89

Perturbation 91

Regret 94

Doubt 97

Hope 100

Comparisons 102

Fear 105

Foreword

By Jeanine Johnson-Smith

First let me say that I am honored and humbled by the request to write the forward for this affirmational collection of poetry and musings. Being a collaborator and writing partner of this author, I have experienced the texture of her words firsthand. I have often been impressed by her use of words and the imagery that she conjures in each of her works. Chevel is a writer that has learned to weave her life experiences into a tapestry of poignant stories and poetry that leave you sometimes to ponder those introspective questions of your own life and experiences. And yet, in those playful moments of reading you chuckle to yourself in recognition of her character's resemblance to your own life.

In the case of Magnificently You, she has matured with vulnerability and empathy in her writing to offer the reader insights into her personal journey. She vacillates between the first person and third person writing style to convey her intimate feelings and life accounts; she then juxtaposes self-acknowledgement with an invitation for the reader to see themselves through the lens of her words. This is surely a book with provoking questions for your journey to self-discovery and self-love.

This book is not about an external view or projection of yourself. This book is for those that have taken courageous steps to embrace their inner child with a desire to heal. These musings are also for those that need a keen jolt of inspiration when life is doing its thing despite your best efforts to control the moments of tribulation. Embracing introspection with care and intention feels like a loving hug for your soul when reading Chevel's words.

With each turn of the page, one can get a sense of the writer. Her life experiences represent the jigsaw puzzle pieces that came together to compile these written expressions. These utterances are thoughtfully conveyed to you with gritty eloquence and transparency woven with a heartfelt empathetic flare. Thus, affording the reader a chance to ponder one's own life for clarity and yet understand Chevel with a curious eye.

I must say I enjoyed these inspirations and musings. The beauty of this literary work is the meaningful bullions of wisdom you will surely comprehend.

"What About Me" begs the question of how you consider yourself in the greater scheme of this world we live in. Or better yet, how you envision yourself in the grand scheme of your own life. There are a billion stories in this world for each person that is still above ground. So "Each day you should be trying to elevate the brand called you."

"WTH" – "The things you are dealing with today were your concerns yesterday."

"Uncomfortable" – Robbing Peter to pay Paul to get Mary off your back." Let this be where you learn the tools to stop this ruinous cycle.

As the reader first and then the reviewer, I realized there is a literary symbiotic relationship between Chevel's inspirational musings. "Hamster Wheel" and "Running" for example gives you a clear and concise view of the life we are living post COVID. We are all running to catch up on what we have missed in that time of stillness. Inside is finally outside and humans are feverishly searching for the next whatever you believe is important.

"Nothingness" had my head trying to wrap around this one line, "Like how do you hug and hold air?" I had to read that three times before it hit me that holding air means breathing deeply into your existence with unabashed hope and faith.

"Tiny Little Invisible Cuts" is by far the most subliminally relevant musing in this book for me. Simply because the words seared into me reflecting on my own life and those tiny little cuts that have scared me over time. Though I have wondered if I am healed or still healing.

In closing, these "drop the mike lines" are proverbs for life if you chose to accept the assignment. Do not let the tape of your life disintegrate without trying these first.

"Regret"

The Japanese proverb says,

"Nana korobi ya oki" which means

"Fall down seven times, get up eight."

"Fear"

Using F.E.A.R in acronym form

"Face Everything and Rise"

ENJOY

Advice

If I do say so myself, I'll give amazing advice.

The problem is I don't follow the advice I give.

I don't believe that I'm worthy.

I don't believe that things are temporary.

I stress over unnecessary things all the time. (Those who know me well are allowed to place an Amen here.)

And although I can give you great advice, what I really need to do is look at that advice.

For me also I guess because it's me giving the advice, I don't hear it the same way.

So, I am hopeful that the words I say to you resonate in your spirits and then your soul.

I proclaim today, I am going to try to make sure that I start listening to me also.

Everything I need I already have. Everything you need. you already have.

Let us always remember that.

You are magnificent just as you are and have to prove nothing to anyone but yourself.

Waiting

I hate waiting.

I am one of the most impatient people you will probably ever meet.

I long to have the patience of a tiger (which is my animal in the Chinese zodiac.)

I don't.

Oftentimes I know things only run on their own time.

I just think sometimes time is a little too slow for me and waiting is hard.

However, waiting for what's next is even harder.

The space between the known and unknown is an uneasy space.

We have to have patience.

I used the word patience because we don't know what tomorrow will bring.

We have no choice on what's going to happen next, when is going to happen, or how it's going to happen.

We have to learn how to shift our energy, learn the balance and how to become okay with waiting.

Some things don't work in the time frame you set.

What's supposed to happen will happen.

Being impatient doesn't help the process.

Real change takes time.

Often waiting offers something better.

I am learning to be grateful in the waiting, as should you.

Waiting means sometimes you pass on something that is merely good and wait for something that is actually great.

<u>*Silence*</u>

Sometimes you have to sit in silence so people can hear you.

There are times when I have been going through and have had very little inspiration to offer.

I had none for myself.

I did not feel wanted or enough.

Inside I was dealing with the many people that sit within me.

I call it being in a cocoon.

I appreciate those who have made me laugh, cry and then made me realize who I am.

That I am more amazing than I dare to believe.

That I am dope just as I am.

Say thanks to all your loved ones, friends and strangers who continue to remind you of who you are.

I was once told to learn to accept the compliments others see in you.

That they see something that you do not.

Be magnificent today.

Remember you are dope.

Even when no one on the outside acknowledges it, let your inside someone speak it.

Growth

I want to grow.

In my mind, body and soul.

I have allowed life's circumstances to
cause me to get sidetracked.

Because of this I am constantly
relearning lessons that I have already
been through.

Continually forgetting that no one can
take away what I know.

Often, I think I live on the brink of
insanity.

Doing the same things, the same way
with my fingers crossed hoping for a
more favorable result.

Is it just me?

Are you hopeful for something that no
matter what, will never come to pass?

Hoping for something that will never be, is like looking at a closed locked door hoping it will open.
We often do that without realizing there is an open one just a few feet away.
It is like a fly buzzing around an open window.
How frustrating is that?
What we need is right there.
We just have to focus and always remember, nothing worth having is easy.
It's our only path to growing into our own unique magnificent selves.
Let's stop buzzing like flies and let's soar like eagles instead.

Intentional

I have a very good friend that often times tells me that they are intentional.

I never asked or questioned what that meant just took it at face value.

The meaning of intentional means deliberate or on purpose.

My thought process was that I thought everyone did things with intention.

Time has shown this is not entirely true.

We do tasks with intentions however do we live our lives with intention?

I'm finding that when you are intentional in all aspects of your life you maneuver differently.

I am realizing that living with
intention means that your every move
is deliberate and with purpose.
It means that you are working towards
a goal or a desired outcome, always.
It means you know where you
eventually want to be and no matter
what you do not allow anything to
alter your intention.
There will be bumps and potholes on
the road to your purpose.
There are supposed to be.
Ask yourself this, when things were
easy did you appreciate them the same
as you did when you had to work for
them?
Live with the intention to always strive
for greatness.

Conviction

What is your conviction?

What is something you stand for?

What is something you will die for

because you believe it so much?

Many will say their children, family,

God.

These are amazing convictions to have

The fact of the matter is many of us,

will not say ourselves.

We don't hold much conviction when

it comes to ourselves.

The meaning of conviction is a fixed

and firm belief.

Do you believe in you?

Do you stand firm in who you are?

Do you stand firm in what you need

for you?

Many of us do not.

We will do everything for everyone
else except for ourselves.
We tend to put ourselves on the side
or on the back burner.
Problem with being on the back
burner or off to side is that you often
forget what you don't readily see.
Do you see you?
Let's be persuaded to put ourselves
first.
Remember that.
Each of us are unique and special.
We all deserve the privilege of
showing up for ourselves.

Why?

Why?

Ever wonder why things happened the
way they did?

Why didn't something go as planned.

Why did it happen to me.

Have you ever asked yourself, why not?

What makes us anymore or any less
special than anyone else?

Don't get me wrong, I do not think I
am better than anyone.

I also don't think anyone is better than
me.

We all go through things and why is
the shortest, hardest question to ask.

What makes any of us think we are
immune to hurt, disappointment or
pain.

We are not.

That fact sucks.

We can live angry about it or we can find productive ways to shift our thought processes.

Instead of asking why me, let's try to just say thank you.

There could have been something much worse on the horizon that we adverted.

A worst fate that wasn't realized.

So instead of why me, embrace each experience good and bad.

It is all part of the journey.

It is a chapter of the book that is you.

Not all chapters are happy however each chapter is necessary in order to write the novel that is you.

Power

Power is often associated with big things.

The definition of power is simply the ability to do or act; capability of doing or accomplishing something.

Every day you arise in power.

The power to get out of bed when the alarm goes off.

The power to get up and take a shower.

The power to cloth yourself.

The power to go to work.

The power to volunteer.

The power to just be.

We tend to forget that there are those that can't do any of these things.

If you can get up and make yourself a meal, that is power.

Learn to embrace the small.

As people we over complicate things.

Live in your ability to just do.

Let simply being who you are be your power.

<u>Random Thoughts</u>

Do you ever get lost in your own thoughts?

I mean thoughts that hold no significant value?

Come on. We all have.

Tell me you haven't wondered if you turned off the iron?

If you locked the door?

Let me ask a question, were you headed to go back home to check?

Were you going to be late to where you were going to go back and check to see?

Do you spend hours thinking about what ifs?

We all have shoulda, coulda, woulda moments.

Always remember that time is something we cannot get back.
Living in shoulda, coulda, woulda solves no problems.
It just causes undo anxiety and concern over things we cannot change.
Focus on what you can change.
Focus on you.
Even if you make mistakes, you are human which is why pencils have erasers.
You are already enough.
Who are you trying to be more for?

Two days

We get so excited over two days.
Most of us work five days grinding at
an office or a grinding at home.
We look forward to those two days.
I hope that in your two days you got
some R&R.
Relaxation and Reflection on what we
need to do next.
This is not a final destination.
We are still processing and going
through this thing called life.
We have all suffered heartbreak.
We have all had moments of
happiness.
And we are hopeful and grateful for
tomorrow.
Two days.
Two days to set a whole week.

Two days to remember us.

Two days to fuel up for the next five.

How are you investing your two days?

<u>What about me?</u>

Have you ever asked yourself that question?

It's like raising your hand to be picked for a game and being overlooked.

It is like jumping up and down and yelling "pick me, pick me".

It is like looking for validation.

No one likes to feel excluded and when we are we start to second guess who we are.

We tend to pick ourselves apart piece by piece.

Know what?

It usually isn't that deep.

Usually, people don't have ulterior motives.

Oh, don't get me wrong sometimes they do, however guess what?

That's none of your business.
It is none of your business how others
feel or think about you.
You are who you are.
You are a work in progress.
Each day you should be trying to
elevate the brand called you.
Will it sometimes hurt?
Absolutely.
You cannot stay there though.
You have work to do.
We get one life, no do overs.
Make it count if for no one else for
you.

WTH!!

Sometimes there are no words.

All you can say is WTH or even WTF
contingent on the situation.

There are things that have no rhyme
or reason.

Life sometimes has you sitting here
like Florida Evans saying Damn,
Damn, Damn.

Asking yourself can I just get a break?

Damn can I just have a moment.

Damn can I just be.

Whether you say WTH or WTF or
even damn can you just be?

Can you just sit in the moment, learn
the lesson and just be.

The things you are dealing with today,
were your concerns yesterday.

Worrying solves nothing.

Why waste time and energy on something that yields no results.

Let's use that energy to focus on something else, ourselves.

Aren't we more important than our what ifs?

Uncomfortable

I've been going though.

Trying to navigate my day to day.

Robbing Peter, to pay Paul, to get
Mary off my back.

Running from here to there for
activities, performances, rehearsals,
hell life.

It is extremely uncomfortable.

It is uncomfortable to survive in the
unknown.

It is uncomfortable to struggle
through the day to day.

In my uncomfortability I am excited
because greater is on the way.

See being comfortable is a temporary
situation.

Comfortability is a place of rest and
relaxation.

Uncomfortability is a place of discomfort.

It is also a place of growth.

Nothing grows in comfort.

Steel is not comfortable when it is being hardened in the fire for strength.

Diamonds are not comfortable going through the pressure to become the beautiful stone it is.

Know that if you are in a season of uncomfortability, it is temporary.

It doesn't feel good and at times it's painful.

Just know that during this process you are being shaped and molded.

You are being prepared for your next level.

Never forget:

YOU HAVE 100% TRACK RECORD OF GETTING OVER BAD DAYS.

So, keep your head up.

Never bow down.

A season of brokenness

I have noticed that this feels like a
season of brokenness.
Life is way harder than it needs to be.
Situations seem more difficult than
they should be.
Be it health, financial, or just even
emotional.
Do you feel like, you are in a spiral
sometimes and it feels like the people
that are connected to you are in their
own spiral too?
Still the great thing about being
broken is that you can be fixed.
Just like growth, brokenness is
uncomfortable.
Sometimes you have to be broken.
Brokenness shows your strength.
Brokenness shows your resilience.

This is a season when things don't
seem to work.
When you're tired and you're tired of
feeling like you have to be all things to
all people.
During your season of brokenness,
learn the lesson that you're being
taught,
Embrace your growth and know that
the better things are on the way.
You got this.
Remember who you are.

<u>*Exhaustion*</u>

Ever been beyond exhausted.
Not tired, exhausted.
They are similar however not the
same.
See tired is defined as exhausted, as by
exertion; fatigued or sleepy.
Exhausted is in the definition however
you have to use energy to get tired.
Exhaustion is to drain of strength or
energy, wear out, or fatigue greatly.
Exhaustion comes from people pulling
from you.
Pulling your energy.
Exhausted means that you are
constantly giving out energy you don't
have to give.
Imagine driving a car.

Now imagine that you run that car every minute of every day.

Eventually the battery will die.

Because all of its energy (battery) has run out.

That's what we do.

We run our batteries until they die.

We have to learn how to plug in and recharge.

We have to allow ourselves to rest.

Resting enables us to store up our energy.

Life is exhausting.

Being is exhausting.

If being exhausted is inevitable, how does one move in exhaustion?

By putting you first.

You matter, you are valued, you are important.

Today let's choose you.

Ambition

A man's achievements should not value
his worth or his purpose.
Ambition is not bad as it is a strong
desire to achieve something through
hard work.
Imagine if you were only valued by
how hard you worked.
How much effort you gave something
or someone.
If you look at society today it is all
about likes, followers and things.
All non-tangible things.
Very rarely about experiences or those
close to you.
It is all about stuff.
Temporary materialistic stuff.

Imagine if tomorrow you no longer
had your stuff, what would you have
left?
Are there people in your life that hold
you accountable?
Are there those that only want to see
you thrive?
Do you have something to bring you
joy?
Joy that is all your own?
Tomorrow is never guaranteed.
Knowing that part, what have you
done for you?
Have you decided that your ambitions
should include you?
That the hard work that you put into
the world should include you also?
Set an ambition for yourself that is
solely for you.
That's not selfish, that's self-care.

Prioritizing yourself allows you to have enough to give others.

<u>F**k around and find out</u>

You know what is the best thing ever? Being underestimated.

See often times people will underestimate your intelligence, your actions, your worth.

These times are when people find themselves in a f*ck around and find out situation.

These moments occur when people make assumptions about you without asking questions.

When they push you too much and too far.

Then you have to show them who you are.

I often say especially when it comes to my children, I am not the one, two, three, four or five.

I love when people say to them "Go get your mom."
My kids always say "Are you sure?"
When people under estimate you it's their ignorance, not yours.
You should not let anyone make you lose your character.
Your character is the "foundation" of who you are.
You should never give anyone the power to affect your foundation.
You would never allow someone to affect where you live and no one should be allowed to affect the house that is you.
There are times when you have to remind people of who you are not and of who you are.
There will always be times when you have to remind people who you are.

There are times when you have to let
people f*ck around and find out just to
remind them who you are.
Make people remember you are not
the one to play around with.

Perception of me

Wonder if I look weak.

Or maybe even helpless.

Otherwise, why would someone that says they love or care for me treat me this way?

Why would they be so apathetic to my feelings and my concerns?

Have you ever asked yourself that question?

Have you ever second guessed your worth based on how someone else perceived you to be?

Did you ever question the why instead of the who?

Did you ever feel like you were not enough.

Maybe you have felt you did not deserve better or could be better.

People will perceive what you portray.
People will treat you the way you allow.
People can only take pieces of you that you are willing to hand out.
You give people the power to treat you the way they do.
People can only do what you allow them to do.
If you demand to be respected and loved, you will receive respect and love.
Never forget who you are and necessitate people to see you and treat you accordingly.
You are unique.
You are genuine.
You are a special edition.
Because there is no one quite like you.

Tiny Little Invisible Cuts

Every time we look past an action or words said, it leaves a tiny little invisible cut on our souls.
After time those tiny little invisible cuts turn into an unseen weeping wound.
Every time we allow someone the power to control us, we are left with a tiny little invisible cut.
Every time we put others above us just to keep the peace, a tiny little invisible cut is left.
Investing time and effort into someone undeserving,
Tiny little invisible cut.
Pouring into someone who isn't pouring into us,
Tiny little invisible cut.

Trying to prove ourselves to those that
don't matter,
Tiny little invisible cut.
Loving someone who is unable to love
you back,
Tiny little invisible cut.
Mistreatment at work,
Tiny little invisible cut.
Ever been told you weren't good
enough, beautiful enough or just not
enough?
Tiny little invisible cut.
Image a paper cut.
It is a tiny cut that hurts a lot.
That is what tiny invisible cuts are.
Tiny means they are hard to see
however they hurt tremendously.
It is those tiny little cuts that hurt
more than we could ever anticipate.
You cannot prevent paper cuts.

You can prevent giving others the ability to leave you with tiny little invisible cuts.

Tiny little invisible cuts slowly tear apart who and what you are.

Each tiny little cut eventually becomes a gaping hole inside of you.

Every time you allow someone to hurt you and you don't respond, you give them the power to leave a tiny little invisible cut.

Strong = Burden

Ask anyone that others say are strong
if they feel like it's a burden.
Always being the strong one is a
burden.
It comes with an inclination that you
are willing to be all things to all
people.
That you can handle every and
anything.
That you never waiver.
That you never collapse.
That you don't have moments of
weakness.
There is no distinctive pattern to
being strong,
It is just a way of handling obstacles
and oftentimes becomes a burden,

A burden because people don't think
you can crack.
You don't break however you do crack.
Small hairline cracks that sit in your
psyche,
Always being told you are strong
becomes a curse,
Sometimes you just want to BE.
Not to be strong,
Not to be soft,
Just BE,
Do I know a lot?
Oh, I know plenty,
You know what knows more?
Google©.
Google© knows way more than you or
I combined.
I do not know all the answers nor do I
want to.

Life should be a never-ending journey
of learning,
Want to know a newly learned lesson?
That being called strong takes away
pieces of your humanity.
See no one ever checks on the strong
one.
You have to be strong for yourself as
you are for everyone else.
Easier said than done.
However always remembering that
nothing worth having is ever easy.

<u>Hamster Wheel</u>

Do you ever feel like you are running
life on a hamster wheel?
You get up,
You shower.
You get ready and dressed,
You either go to work, drop off kids,
care for others or all of the above.
You then come home,
Eat, shower, sleep and the next day
repeat.
Sometimes you are so tired from life
you don't eat or sleep,
You can't see any end because you are
running in a perpetual circle.
Wash, Rinse, Repeat.
All without taking a breath.
When is the last time you breathed?

I mean if you are reading this you are breathing, but how long has it been since you took a breath and breathed? Filled your lungs with air and exhaled? Exhaled the frustrations. Exhaled the disappointments. Exhaled the fears. Funny thing about hamsters on a hamster wheel? Even they stop and take rest breaks.

<u>*Time*</u>

365 Days, 1,440 minutes, 86,400 seconds.

Do I think that I am amazing? Absolutely.

Do I know that I am the things that dreams are made of?

YES!!

You will never know how long it took for me to say this.

Those in my inner circle know that day in and day out I have struggled.

I struggled with not feeling like enough.

With feeling unworthy.

We all have feelings of doubt.

Of feelings of insecurity.

Of feeling that failure is final.

None of the above is true.

Everything takes one hour, one minute, one second.
We get 86,400 seconds a day.
Most times you have to break it down to the bare minimum.
We often look at the big picture that we don't see the small things.
Like you are a rockstar if you even put on clothes today.
Small things add up.
Always remember: How do you eat an elephant?
One piece at a time.
Life is one day at a time, one hour at a time, one minute at a time, one second....
At a time.

<u>*Masterpiece*</u>

You are a masterpiece.
Carefully crafted from the very top of
your head to the bottom of your feet.
There is nothing about you that is not
by design.
Just at your very core you are unique.
Special simply because you are YOU.
There is no one in the world that is
you.
Even if you are a multiple, a twin, a
triplet, etc.
Only you are YOU.
Your personality is yours.
Your pain is yours.
Your fears are yours.
Your triumphs are yours.
Everything about you is a unique
masterpiece.

More exquisite than the Mona Lisa.

More divine than Michelangelo.

More intricate than the Sistine
Chapel.

Remember to always remember to
treat yourself as such.

Always remember you are more
valuable than any piece of art you can
hang on a wall.

YOU are a masterpiece who should
never discount your value.

There in nothing, no one more
valuable than YOU.

Never forget that.

Begging

Why do we beg so much?

Begging the wrong person to love us.

Begging to be seen for who we are.

Begging to be acknowledged.

Begging for all we don't currently
have and perceive we need.

Begging denotes a need.

So, when we beg for all of these things
what do we get in return?

Do we get the wrong person to love
us?

Is that a prize? A reward?

To be loved by the person who is not
fully our person?

To be seen by individuals who hold no
value in our lives. Whose only goal is
to get what they can from you.

You will never have to beg for what is
rightfully yours.
It will be given to you willingly with
no ill will attached to it.
Have you ever begged for something
and it turned out to be the worst thing
ever?
You have everything you need right
now.
It might not be what you want
however it is everything you need in
the moment.
It is part story of you.
Not every chapter will be glorious,
some will be downright horrible.
No matter what it is your journey and
you are not required to beg for what is
rightfully already yours.
No need to beg, you are enough just as
you are.

<u>Control is a façade</u>

Being in control is a façade.

The definition of control is the power to influence or direct people's behavior or the cause of events.

Do you have control over how others react to you?

Do you have control over the outcome of certain situations in your life?

There is no control in a universe that is uncertain.

Everything you go through, been through and will go through has already been designed.

The ugly, just okay, good and great have already been written in the book that is you.

Could you have stopped the bad things that have happened?

Ponder this, if the bad thing didn't happen would the good thing have happened?

We always want to control how things will be or are.

Sometimes bad things have to occur to make room for the good to come through.

Understand not all bad things need to happen, unfortunately it is just the way life is designed.

No one wants to be in the midst of a storm.

However too much sunshine creates a desert.

You need the rain in order for the flowers to grow.

Just like you cannot control if the storm will come, you also cannot control the beauty of the flowers that will grow.

Nothingness

Sometimes there are no words of
wisdom to or encouragement to
impart.
Sometimes in our nothingness we
learn our biggest lessons.
Stillness is uncomfortable however
necessary.
It is in the stillness and complete
nothingness that you see everything
you looked past.
You start to see the small or a minutia.
Truthfully because you have no choice.
The things we would normally look
past.
Nothingness hurts.
Feeling devoid is a heavy feeling.
It leaves you restless because there is
nothing.

No answers no rhyme, no reason.
Just nothing.
Hard to embrace nothing.
Like how do you hug and hold air.
However just like air, just because you
cannot see it does not mean it doesn't
exist.
Just like in your nothingness there are
things there that you needed to
acknowledge and just were unable to.
Nothingness is another stage in your
journey.
Learn to find the lessons being taught
in your nothingness and stillness.
It is important so you can see all the
things you were too busy with life to
notice.

Grace

Allow yourself some grace in your weak moments.

We offer others grace when the have their "off" moments.

Are we not allowed to do that for ourselves?

We assist people in need either personally, or with altruistic intention.

We give favor to those who do not deserve it.

We give "passes" to those who need to be held accountable.

We allow people the space to breathe.

Do we allow ourselves rest?

Do we give ourselves a "pass" when we are less than perfect?

Don't we deserve grace?

Aren't we allowed "off" moments too?

Today at some point allow yourself
some grace.
Instead of beating yourself for what
you could not do, praise all that you
have already done.
You deserve grace to breathe too.

Backwards

There is a story in the Bible most know.

It is about a man named Lot and how he was instructed to leave a place and not to look back.

Lot did not look back, however his wife did and turned into a pillar of salt.

How many of us would turn into a pillar of salt?

How many of us are focused on what's behind us?

Living in the possibility of something as opposed to the truth of what is reality.

Now looking backwards to what you left is fruitless.

However, there are times you have to
go backwards.
There are times that feel like you are
moving in reverse.
While looking backwards makes you
lose focus,
Moving backwards helps you elevate
and see things differently.
There are times when backwards helps
you focus on what's ahead.
You lost the job, car, house.
All feels lost however when you look
ahead there is better ahead.
You cannot do anything about what
you no longer have,
You can focus on what you need to do
to be ready for better.
Always remember if your hands are
holding on to something, they are not
open to receive better.

Clutter

When your life is cluttered, your mind
is cluttered.
You tend to run in circles from one
task to the next.
When we are not organized in our
lives, we are definitely not organized
in our minds.
Our minds tend to be full.
Always thinking.
Always solving problems.
Always just trying to survive life.
Often worrying about the what ifs yet
to come.
That's why it takes us forever to finish
the simplest tasks.
You just keep putting it off.
Too busy binge watching the show you
have already seen all the episodes for.

There is nothing wrong with decompressing however did you do what you promised yourself you would do.
Did you start that business?>
Did you write that book?
What about that idea you have been promising to implement?
When our mind is cluttered, we tend to make excuses about why we can't.
Can't is a made-up word.
You can do anything if you put your mind and effort into it.
When you say you can't do something you have already resigned yourself it's not doable.
How about we try and take the first step.
Take a hint from babies.

They understand the process of the journey.

You have to first roll over.

Then you have to crawl.

Then you take your first step.

Then you run.

It takes you taking that first step.

It is better for your mind to be cluttered with new ideas to implement, then the possibilities that will never be realized.

Heavy

Martin Luther King Jr. said "A man can't ride your back unless it's bent".
Carrying anything on your back becomes heavy after a while.
Carrying others on your back or even on your shoulders is heavy.
Not physically carrying them however mentally carrying them.
Carrying other people's burdens and problems, can be downright crippling.
We tend to carry the burdens of those we love.
We want to make it better; we want to fix it.
Doesn't matter what the it is, just it.
Eventually carrying all of that "baggage" of others on our backs.

Imagine carrying a refrigerator on your back.

That is what happens internally when you carry everyone else's problems as your own.

It becomes very heavy on your being and in your psyche when you do that.

We have to learn that No is a complete sentence.

Saying no does not make you a bad person it makes you an individual who has put themselves first.

Release some of that heaviness one bag at a time.

Walking around bent over from all that you are carrying means you can't see straight ahead.

When you move bent over you can only see a few steps in front of yourself.

How do you see the horizon if you are bent over looking at the ground.
Today stand upright and look ahead.
When you can't hold anymore emotional baggage, learn to tell others no.
If no one else choses you, you chose YOU.

Running

Does it feel like you are always
running?
Running to and fro all the time.
Repeatedly moving from one place to
another and then back again.
Like you are running in circles.
Guess what?
Running in circles leaves you running
in a continual loop.
A circle has no start or end point it
just goes around and around.
Running without a set destination or
solution is just running in a circle.
There are times where you have to
stop running and pause.
Pause to think of a possible solution to
a problem.

Pause to see an opportunity that
resides outside of the circle.
Pause to remember who you are and
what you need to do for you.
Running in circles does nothing but
wear you out.
Eventually you will burn out and wear
a hole in the fabric that is you.
You wouldn't walk around in holey
clothes.
Why would you walk around with
holes in you?

Energy

Energy is simply the ability to do work.

Everything has energy.

Money has energy as it does work when you spend it.

It is working.

Energy also has negative impacts.

Have you ever been in a good mood and a negative person comes around and it makes you then be in a foul mood?

Yep, it is their energy.

Energy shifts from thing to thing and from person to person.

If someone is going through something and you give them a hug it helps shift their energy.

We should all try and remember that
our energy affects those we encounter.
You should always protect your
energy.
Not for others but for yourself.
You should not let anyone who doesn't
have good intentions pull from your
energy.

Perturbation

Perturbation is the action of perturbing: the state of being perturbed.

Perturbed means to feel anxiety or concern or be unsettled.

While perturbation is a noun, perturbed is an adjective.

It originates from the Latin word perturbare which means to disturb greatly.

All these definitions to say that many of us are living in perturbation.

We feel anxious over things that are unfamiliar.

We are unsettled when things do not go our way.

We are concerned when we can't control things or outcomes.

Know what the opposites of
perturbation are?
Calm, Peace, Quiet, Composure.
Here in the US, they teach the
children in kindergarten, "You get
what you get and you don't get upset."
Easy when you are five.
Not so much when you are 25, 35,
45.......
What do you do when life gets in the
way?
Do you get anxious, angry or
perturbed?
Why?
What could you have changed?
Are you certain that if you changed
whatever its is would it give a more
favorable result?
Everything is not for everybody.
You have to learn to be okay with that.

Oftentimes our rewards come in different packaging.
Just because it doesn't have a bright shiny bow on it, will you not accept it?

Regret

My great grandmother always used to say "if you regret doing something, you had no business doing it."
That is easier said than done.
There are plenty of things I ended up regretting.
Regretting dating that individual.
Regret having children with that individual.
Regret moving far from those you love.
Regret taking that job.
Regret wearing that outfit.
Regret choosing that friend.
Regret usually comes about when we made a choice, we wish we didn't make.

Regret also comes when we made a choice and the outcome was not what we foresaw.

Living in regret will also lead way to you feeling like you failed or are a failure.

Just because your choice/decision didn't yield the results you wanted you don't have to regret them.

Did you learn the lesson?

Did you process the end result.

Did you figure out what you can do differently.

Funny thing about failure is if you take the F and turn it sideways, it becomes a step.

A step up.

Never forget that if you are failing, then you are trying.

Don't live in regret.

The Japanese proverb says,
"Nana korobi ya oki" which means
'Fall down seven times, get up eight'.
Don't regret the fall down, regret the
fact if you never get back up.

Doubt

Doubt means to be uncertain.

To be unsure and to lack confidence.

To be afraid.

What are you fearful about?

Are you afraid to start over?

Are you afraid to allow people to see the genuineness of you?

Are you afraid you aren't good enough?

Do you even doubt why you are even here?

Do you doubt that you deserve love?

When you doubt you tend not to make decisions.

We tend to second guess everything that we do.

We often need to have proof that everything will be okay.

How can we prove that nothing bad will happen?

We cannot.

Living in doubt is a negative reinforcement and intensifies fear.

Living in fear has us second guessing each step, each move.

It takes everything positive and turns it into a negative reaction.

Do they really like me?

Do they love me for me or for what I can do for them?

Am I really talented or is this just luck?

Do I really deserve all the things being given to me?

Or as simple as am I pretty/handsome enough to have someone?

Am I really a good person or are they just being nice?

Living in doubt is a stagnant process.
You can not grow if you motionless.
You are basically lifeless.
How can you live life if there is no life
to live?
This is the only life you get.
You can't go back and change
anything that has already been done.
This is your one life, no do overs.

<u>*Hope*</u>

There are times when things get tough.
There are times when things get down right horrible and difficult.
Through it all, you have to have hope.
Hope will allow you to know that everything will eventually be okay.
Through the process you have to believe that there is always better on the horizon.
That no matter what you are going to be okay.
That you are more than capable.
That you have more strength than you believe.
You have to see beyond your circumstances.

Have the hope that you are more than worthy.

If you remember nothing else, remember you are already more than enough.

Have hope that it is an honor to know you and that no matter what you are going through, everything will eventually be alright.

Have the hope that the process will bring you to where you need to be.

Comparisons

Every day we compare ourselves to others.

It's inevitable, especially in the world.

Am I pretty enough?

Am I tall enough?

Am I skinny enough?

Am I thick enough?

Am I successful?

Do they like me?

Do they love me?

All day long a thought similar to the above crosses our minds.

And when social media is involved, it makes it so much worse.

Would it help if you feel better if you knew that beautiful girl with the "perfect" body and amazing makeup was actually using the makeup to cover up

the fact that her boyfriend beats his
insecurities on her daily?
Or that the man with the amazing Maserati and penthouse apartment goes
home lonely every night to an empty
home.
Our society breeds and helps grow our
own insecurities.
The insecurities we think we hide even
though they shine through.
Comparing does nothing.
It solves no problems, and the truth is
comparison is the thief of joy.
You cannot have joy if you are continually comparing what you don't have
or what you think you lack.
Instead of comparing how about we
try to embrace how unique and authentic you are.

All the things that make you,
The you that only you can be.

Fear

We all have fears.

Some fear heights,

Some fear rodents or insects.

Some fear being alone.

Often, we hear sayings that fear is

false evidence appearing real.

My fear of rats is real, and I am unsure

if that is false.

In all seriousness I also heard two

other variations of fear.

Face everything and run. If a rat is

involved I might do just that.

The other was Face everything and

rise.

For me this means no matter what you

think you cannot do, face it and still

rise above.

You cannot help what didn't happen.

You cannot help what couldn't happen.

What you can do is figure out what is next and how to move forward with what is right at this moment.

You cannot live in fear of what is to come because the future isn't guaranteed.

You cannot live in fear of something that has happened because that is the past and you cannot go back and change the past.

What you can do is figure out what you can do to succeed.

How do you face everything, the good bad and ugly and rise above?

How do you rise beyond what you ever thought you could?

Imagine if instead of walking afraid you walked with purpose.

You walked knowing that each day you opened your eyes you were destined to do something wonderful. No matter how big or small it might be.

www.ingramcontent.com/pod-product-compliance
Lightning Source LLC
Chambersburg PA
CBHW061549310726
48972CB00008B/2683